Make It Three

The Story of the CSS *H. L. Hunley*
Civil War Submarine

MAKE IT THREE

The Story of the CSS *H. L. Hunley*
Civil War Submarine

Margie Willis Clary

with original illustrations by
Becky Hyatt Rickenbaker

SANDLAPPER PUBLISHING CO., INC.

Second Printing, 2003

Published by Sandlapper Publishing Co., Inc.
Orangeburg, South Carolina 29115

Manufactured in the United States of America

Library of Congress Cataloging-in-Publication Data

Clary, Margie Willis, 1931–
     Make it three : the story of the CSS H.L. Hunley, Civil War submarine / by
Margie Willis Clary ; with illustrations by Becky Hyatt Rickenbaker.
          p. cm.
     Includes bibliographical references.
     Summary: When Josh visits Charleston, South Carolina, he becomes
fascinated with the history of the Confederate submarine, H.L. Hunley, which
sank a Union ship in 1864, and he, his mother, and aunt move to Charleston
in time for the raising of the submarine out of the sea.
     ISBN 0-87844-158-1
     1. H.L. Hunley (Submarine)—Juvenile fiction. 2. United States—
History—Civil War, 1861-1865—Juvenile fiction. [1. H.L. Hunley (Submarine)—Fiction. 2. United States—History—Civil War, 1861-1865—Fiction.
3. Submarines—History—Fiction. 4. Aunts—Fiction. 5. Underwater
archaeology—Fiction. 6. Moving, Household—Fiction. 7. Charleston
(S.C.)—Fiction.] I. Rickenbaker, Becky, ill. II. Title.

PZ7.C5627 Mak 2001
[Fic]—dc21
                                                            2001020659

Dedicated to

**my grandchildren
Caleb, Jill, and Scott**

~ ~ ~

A *special dedication to*

Friends of the Hunley,
Charleston, South Carolina

~ ~ ~

Special thanks to

Timmy Gunter and Scott Clary,
who served as models for Josh

Wayne Clary of Goose Creek,
who provided some of the photographs

and

Dawn Hammer Davis,
park ranger, Ft. Moultrie,
who assisted with the story's historical accuracy

Contents

1. The Trip to Charleston

2. Discovering the *Hunley*

3. The Submarine's History

4. The Charleston Museum

5. More to See

6. The Sidewalk Cafe

7. The *Hunley* Museum

8. Further Exploration

9. Magnolia Cemetery

10. Grandpa Cooper

11. The Graves of the *Hunley* Crews

12. The Ghost

13. A Rainy Day

14. Fort Moultrie

15. Another *Hunley*

16. Rest for the Weary

17. Aunt Louise Moves In

18. The New House

19. Moving Day

20. The *Hunley* Comes Home

Make It Three

The Story of the CSS *H. L. Hunley*
Civil War Submarine

PART I

Chapter 1
THE TRIP TO CHARLESTON
April 2000

The light of early dawn brightened the window of the hotel room where Josh, Mom, and Aunt Louise slept. The alarm of a clock pierced the silence.

Jumping up, Josh called, "It's time to go sightseeing."

Aunt Louise rolled over and turned off the alarm, murmuring, "Don't be in such a hurry, Josh. It's early."

The three had driven to Charleston the night before. Mom came to the city to attend a nursing conference at the medical center. Aunt Louise would keep Josh company.

Aunt Louise was especially glad to visit Charleston. The city felt like home. She had worked at the navy shipyard for thirty-five years, until 1994. She loved the area and was delighted to be asked to accompany the two as

Josh's personal tour guide.

At retirement, Aunt Louise had moved to Union to be near Mom and Josh. She was a favorite aunt and spent as much time as possible with her only living relatives.

Aunt Louise was the oldest person Josh had ever known. She wore big thick glasses that magnified her eyes. Her hands were wrinkled, and big blue veins wiggled beneath the skin when she moved her fingers. Outside, she always wore lace-up boots and a hat. She collected stamps, planted flowers, wrote letters, and read books. She particularly liked to read about the Civil War at Charleston. She told lots of stories—funny stories, family stories, and history stories. Josh always had a great time when Aunt Louise was around.

On the ride to Charleston, Aunt Louise told Josh the story of the *Isaac P. Smith*, a Union gunboat captured January 28, 1863, on the Stono River. The account was a family story as well as a history story. Aunt Louise's great-grandfather witnessed the capture and wrote home about it. Josh had heard this story before, but he loved his aunt's tales no matter how many times she told them.

Aunt Louise seemed to know everything about the Civil War at Charleston, and this first morning in the city Josh was anxious to go sightseeing so she could tell him more.

"Come on, Aunt Louise," he cried. "Please, get up!"

Aunt Louise sat up, rubbed her eyes, and stretched her arms high above her head. Reaching for her glasses, she said, "What's the rush? We've got all day."

"I know, but I don't want to waste a minute."

Aunt Louise threw back the covers and slid her feet into the waiting bedroom slippers.

"Well, get dressed and wake up Sylvia," she said, as she closed the bathroom door.

Josh dressed in haste, then walked to the bed where his mom was sleeping.

Shaking her by the shoulder, he yelled, "It's time to get up, Mom! Aunt Louise and I are almost ready to go."

"Hold it down, Son," Mom muttered in reply. "I know you're excited, but most historical places aren't open this early."

Without another word, Mom rubbed her sleepy eyes and rose from the bed.

Aunt Louise appeared, dressed, and gave Mom an understanding wink. As Mom slipped into the bathroom to dress for the day, Aunt Louise put on her hat and crossed to the window. She could see lazy, early-

morning Market Street, not yet filled with tourists. Beyond the vendors' stalls, the United States Custom House stood quiet. A ship was anchored in the harbor. The sun, just peeping over the horizon, cast red and yellow beams across the water.

"Come here, Josh." Aunt Louise motioned him across the room. "I want you to see a real Charleston sunrise."

Josh ran to the window. Looking toward the harbor, he exclaimed, "Wow, the sun is so red it's making the water different colors. Are *all* sunrises in Charleston like this?"

"Not all of them," Aunt Louise answered, "*but all the ones I remember.*"

Josh pressed his nose against the glass to get a better view. "I think I'll remember this one," he said. "It's awesome."

At that moment Mom came back into the room, dressed and ready to go.

"Where to first?" asked Josh.

Mom picked up her purse and briefcase. "First, we go downstairs and eat breakfast," she said.

Aunt Louise patted her stomach. "Good. I'm hungry. We can make our plans at the breakfast table, Josh."

"Great idea." Josh raced out the door and ran ahead to the elevator.

On the first floor, the dining room was already filled with diners.

"Are all of these people tourists?" asked Josh.

"Could be," answered Aunt Louise, "*but so are we.*"

While they waited for a table, Aunt Louise browsed through tourist brochures on display. She picked out several that gave information about historical sites in the city and dropped them into her purse just as the waiter signaled their table was ready.

Josh ate his breakfast in a rush, talking the whole time. "Have you decided where we'll go first?"

"I think we'll start at the Charleston Museum," Aunt Louise answered. "It's the oldest public museum in the United States—and it's a great one."

Mom rose from her seat and picked up her briefcase. "No better place to begin. I wish I could go with you. But I've got to run—can't be late. I'll see you around 1:00 at the Sidewalk Cafe."

"Fine, dear," responded Aunt Louise. "Have a good day."

Stopping at the cashier's desk, Mom paid the check and left.

Aunt Louise raised her cup, planning to leisurely finish her coffee. But Josh was in such a tear to get started, she declined another cup and they headed out.

Chapter 2
DISCOVERING THE *HUNLEY*

The April morning was warm and sunny, so the two decided to walk to the museum. Up Meeting Street they went. The smell of blooming wisteria vines filled the air. Pigeons pecked along the sidewalk. Josh scooted ahead, stopping here and there to admire the aged buildings and the large churches.

"There's nothing like springtime in Charleston," Aunt Louise remarked.

As they passed Marion Square, Josh asked about the hotel there that looked like a fort.

"That's the old Citadel," Aunt Louise explained. "It *is* built like a fortress. It was used for years as the campus of South Carolina's military college. Your uncle Joseph went to school there. The campus is now located on the Ashley River. That's another place we must visit someday. It has its own museum—and lots of history.

"How much farther do we have to walk?" asked Josh.

"About a block. You can see it from here." Aunt Louise pointed ahead as she spoke.

Josh bolted forward, stopping at the traffic light to wait for Aunt Louise. Together they crossed the street to the Charleston Museum.

The first thing Josh saw was a submarine displayed out front. A sign hanging from its torpedo read, "Replica, Confederate Submarine *H. L. Hunley*. Story inside Museum."

At first sight, Josh was intrigued. He examined the vessel from one end to the other.

"Say, isn't this the same sub we've been hearing about on television? And Miss Adams brought some newspaper articles about it to class."

"Yes, it is," Aunt Louise replied. "It's been in the news lately because the remains of the original *Hunley* were discovered not far from here, just off Sullivan's Island. They're hoping to bring it to the surface by 2001. Just think, it won't be long until we can see the real thing."

Rubbing his hands along the side of the iron vessel, Josh asked, "Is this how it really looked?"

"As best we know. The replica was built to scale by men who have done tremendous research on the vessel. However, the diving crew that discovered the original sub seems to think it had more parts and may be more refined than this one. We'll just have to wait until it's brought to the surface to find out."

"It looks different from the submarines they use today," Josh said.

"It is different. Today's submarines are much more streamlined," Aunt Louise answered. "The *Hunley* was the first submarine to ever sink a warship in battle. It sank the Union ship *Housatonic* in 1864. But the *Hunley* mysteriously disappeared after the attack. It was thought to have been destroyed—until its discovery in 1995."

"The sign says 'story inside.' Let's go." Josh moved toward the entrance. "I want to tell Miss Adams about this when I get home."

"Wait a minute," Aunt Louise called, shuffling through the many brochures in her purse. "Here's a pamphlet that tells about the CSS *Hunley*. See, there's a picture of it on the front. Sit. Let's read what it has to say before we go inside."

Chapter 3
THE SUBMARINE'S HISTORY

The two sat down on a bench near the museum's entrance. Opening the brochure, Aunt Louise began to read, "'The *H. L. Hunley* submarine was designed by James McClintock and Baxter Watson. A third man, Horace Hunley, a lawyer and planter from New Orleans, joined the effort and provided much of the money for the construction of this unique underwater vessel.

"'The submarine was built in Mobile, Alabama. Created from an old steam boiler, its hull was cone shaped and the middle body was a cylinder, ten feet long. The vessel, measuring approximately forty feet in length, was designed to be powered manually by eight men turning a crank connected to a small, spiral propeller. A ninth crew member would serve as captain. Operating at full power, the vessel could travel at a speed of four knots per hour. About seventeen feet from where the crew sat, a torpedo was attached to a pine spar extending from the bow of the vessel.'"

"Yeah, see that torpedo on the replica. That's mighty close to the crew," Josh exclaimed. "What else does it say?"

Aunt Louise continued, "'Once the vessel submerged, the crew had no supply of fresh oxygen and only a candle to give light. Underwater, with the hatches latched, there was no way to escape. In reality, the *Hunley* was a deathtrap. Thirteen men died in two separate accidents before it was used in battle. Horace Hunley lost his life in a test run. He and his crew are buried in Magnolia Cemetery in Charleston, South Carolina.'"

"Can we go to the cemetery?" interrupted Josh.

"Maybe," answered Aunt Louise, "if we have time. Here, why don't you finish reading the brochure."

Taking the brochure from Aunt Louise, Josh read, "'It was reported that during fall and winter of 1863-64 of the Civil War the *Hunley* prowled the waters of Charleston Harbor. Sighted surfacing for air, it was at times referred to as 'The Porpoise.'

"'On the night of February 17, 1864, the *Hunley*, manned by eight crew members and Lieutenant George Dixon surprised the USS *Housatonic*, which was part of the blockade in Charleston Harbor. The *Hunley*'s torpedo sank the *Housatonic*. It was reported that five members of the ship's crew drowned, but the twenty-one officers and 137 other sailors were rescued by a nearby gunboat. The *Hunley* seemed to disappear in the explosion. Neither its nine members nor the vessel were ever found.'"

Josh stopped reading and looked up. "That's not true anymore. It has been found."

"That's correct," replied Aunt Louise, "but that brochure was printed before they discovered the *Hunley*. Read on."

"'The *Hunley* became the first submarine to sink an enemy ship during wartime. A memorial to the crew members who lost their lives during the training operations was erected in 1889, a gift from the United Daughters of the Confederacy. The monument is located in White Point Gardens at the tip of the Charleston peninsula.'

"Geez!" Josh exclaimed, handing the brochure to Aunt Louise. "Those men had *some* adventure handling that submarine. I would have been scared to get into such a tiny space with only a candle for light. That's too weird."

"You couldn't have gotten me in there either," said

Aunt Louise, returning the brochure to her purse. "Those men weren't just adventurers, though. They were pioneers for underwater vessels."

"Pioneers?" Josh questioned. "You mean, like the people who went west to settle our country?"

"A pioneer is anyone who is willing to venture or lead the way into new places or new opportunities," Aunt Louise explained. "Many lives were lost in the

Hunley, but much was learned from the fatal efforts of those brave men. The *Hunley* was a forerunner for the submarines of today."

Josh ran back to the replica. He rubbed his hands over the hatch, the hull, and the bow. He peeked inside through the glass window and imagined sailors sitting there. It was eerie to think about being closed inside without fresh air.

He raced to where Aunt Louise sat. "And just think," he said, "they have finally found the *Hunley*. I wonder if it will look like this one."

"It will take a long time to make it look like that," Aunt Louise replied. "It's been underwater over a century."

"There will be barnacles on it for sure!" Josh said.

"It will be rusted and corroded," added Aunt Louise. "The job to restore it will be difficult, but they're going to try." Aunt Louise rose from the bench. "Maybe we can learn about the recovery as we tour the museum. I seem to remember a display of the *Hunley* from way back. Let's move on. We have much to see before lunch."

"Forward!" Josh shouted. He gave the vessel one last rub and ran to the entrance where Aunt Louise was waiting.

As Josh and Aunt Louise walked through the doors of the museum, Josh said, "We have just begun our tour and I'm already learning history. Won't Mom be amazed?"

Aunt Louise laughed. "She will be, but I'm not sure if she can live with *two* history buffs around."

Josh's eyes sparkled. "She'll get used to it." Then he frowned suddenly. "I wish Mom liked history."

"Oh, but she does," Aunt Louise said.

"Why doesn't she ever talk to me about it?" asked Josh.

"Josh, your mom has been so busy working and going to school to get her nursing degree, she hasn't had much free time. She really liked history when she was your age. She used to come and visit me here in Charleston and we'd go sightseeing. We went to Fort Sumter one summer. She really had a good time. You'll have to ask her about it."

"You bet I will," Josh said, pushing open the second door.

Chapter 4
THE CHARLESTON MUSEUM

Aunt Louise bought tickets as Josh studied the animal skeleton hanging from the ceiling.

"Whoa!" Josh squealed. "Look at that. Is it a dinosaur?"

"No, it's a whale," Aunt Louise said. "It was captured off the coast of South Carolina back in 1800."

"Mom was right. This is a good place to start sightseeing. Old museum, here we come!"

As they walked toward the stairs, Josh spied a poster of the *Hunley* on display. The caption beneath the image gave a brief historical sketch.

"Yep, there's more about the *Hunley* here. This says the *Hunley* was found in 1995 'by a diving expedition led by novelist and undersea explorer Clive Cussler. The submarine was sighted off Sullivan's Island, not far from where it went down after sinking the *Housatonic*.' To think, it was lost for 131 years."

"It is exciting to think it will finally be coming home," Aunt Louise said, as she turned to go up the steps. "The lady at the ticket booth said there's a video about the *Hunley* on the second floor, and the next showing is in five minutes."

"But I want to see the other exhibits," Josh groaned.

"We will," Aunt Louise said, "but let's watch the video first. We should still have time to take in more of the museum after the show."

At the top of the stairs, arrows along the wall led to the *Hunley* Corner. They had no trouble recognizing the space. An encased model of the submarine was displayed on a stand by the left wall. On the right wall hung a large photograph of the *Hunley*, with crewmen standing beside it. Next to the picture was a framed map of Charleston Harbor; a star designated the spot where the old vessel sits on the ocean floor. A television monitor was positioned in the back corner of the triangular space where the two walls joined.

"There's great enthusiasm around here about the raising of the *Hunley*," Aunt Louise said. "Just look at how many people are here to watch the video."

"There aren't enough seats," Josh whispered. "I'll

sit on the floor."

Aunt Louise managed to squeeze onto a bench just as the video began.

The tape related the story of the *H.L. Hunley* from its creation in Mobile, Alabama, to its discovery in the Charleston Harbor in 1995. According to the narrator, General Pierre Gustave Tousant Beauregard wanted the *Hunley* brought to Charleston. He believed an underwater vessel would improve the defense of the city. Actors portrayed General Beauregard, James McClintock, Baxter Watson, Horace Hunley, and other crew members, bringing the scenes to life.

Writer and historian Mark Ragan described the submarine's first training disaster during which five crew members drowned. These five were buried in a cemetery for Confederate sailors. The cemetery was effaced in 1947 during the building of the Johnson Hagood Stadium on the Citadel campus.

Josh began to rap his fingers on the floor. He was eager to continue the tour of the museum, and the forty-five-minute video seemed awfully long. His eyes wandered to a display of Confederate swords hanging on the wall. He wanted to go over and touch them. Were these very swords used to fight the enemy? he wondered.

The sound of a familiar name forced Josh to snap

out of his daydream. He looked up at the monitor. "A dive team funded by American explorer and author Clive Cussler," the narrator was saying, "discovered the *Hunley* in May 1995 submerged in sand four miles offshore and thirty feet beneath the water's surface, not far from where it went down in 1864.

"Tests show the submarine is partly intact but has faced much deterioration. Due to the danger of further decline, the *Hunley* must be kept wet after it is brought to the surface and loaded for transport. It will be taken by barge to Building 255, an old warehouse at the now-closed Charleston navy base. It must remain cool and unexposed to outside air during the restoration. Hopefully the public will be able to view the process.

"It is projected the submarine will be raised from the ocean floor by the year 2001. Plans are underway to construct a building at the Charleston Museum to house the submarine after it is restored. The building will serve as an exhibit hall for artifacts and a home for the submarine. The cost to raise and restore the submarine is estimated at more than twenty million dollars."

"Oh, man!" Josh thought. "That's a lot of money!"

Music began to play and Josh realized the video was over. He stood and stretched. "Good video, but too long," he said.

"Yes," replied Aunt Louise. "A little repetitious, having read the brochure, but it did a thorough job of telling the whole *Hunley* story."

Josh stood silent for a moment. "To think," he said, "those last nine sailors might still be in the sub when it's brought up."

"It's a fascinating story," Aunt Louise responded, adding softly, "but a sad one too. The *Hunley* was definitely a deathtrap from the beginning."

Chapter 5
MORE TO SEE

Aunt Louise looked at her watch. "Good gracious! Is it twelve o'clock already? We'll have to hurry. I want you to see the Egyptian mummy. It's been in this museum at least fifty years. I've seen it many times, but I always want to see it again."

As they walked through the bird habitats toward the Egyptian exhibit, Aunt Louise took out another brochure.

"Here, Josh. This tells about the mummy and the rest of the Egyptian display. You can keep it to share with your classmates."

"Thanks," Josh said, then he ran ahead to find the mummy.

By the time Aunt Louise reached the Egyptian display, Josh was ready to move on.

"What do we see now?" he asked.

"I was hoping we would find more on the *Hunley's* recovery. I'll ask someone."

She waved to a museum guide. "I was wondering if there is more information here about the *H. L. Hunley*, besides what's in the *Hunley* Corner."

"The museum owns many items pertaining to the submarine: maps, dioramas, scaled replicas, original construction plans, a knife and a revolver from that period, and artists' drawings," the guide said. "For the past few years, however, these treasures have been stored away. They're being refurbished now for display in the new building that will be constructed to house the recovered *Hunley*. I'm sorry they're not available for you to see at this time. There are several books in our gift shop that contain pictures of the original submarine and the inventors. Your young man might enjoy one of them."

"Thank you," Aunt Louise said. "We hope to come again when the new building is completed."

"We'll be glad to have you," replied the guide. "By the way, there is a full-length movie entitled *The Hunley*, which was recently shown on Turner Network Television. It was filmed in Charleston. It is now available on videotape. You would enjoy it I'm sure."

"I'm glad to know about the movie. We'll be on the

lookout for it. Thanks again." Aunt Louise moved quickly to catch up with Josh.

She found him in the hands-on room, staring up at the polar bear. "The guide said there are books in the gift shop about the *Hunley*," she said.

"Can I buy one?" he asked. "Then Mom can see the pictures and read about the *Hunley* for herself."

Aunt Louise opened her purse and pulled a twenty-dollar bill from her wallet. "Here, take this. The gift shop is at the bottom of the steps. Go on down and pick out a book. I want to see the Old South exhibit before I descend."

Josh took two steps at a time getting to the gift shop. Skidding to a stop in front of the glass case, his eyes quickly scanned the displays. He spied a book about the *Hunley* and another on submarine history. Thumbing through them both, he chose the one that gave the history of submarines in America. It included a chapter about the *Hunley*.

"May I help you?" the clerk asked.

"Yes, I'll take this book," Josh replied.

"So you're interested in submarines, are you?" she asked.

"Yes, especially the *Hunley*," he answered. "I can't wait to see it when it's brought to the surface."

"That won't be long now. They're saying they will begin work on it by this summer. Isn't that exciting?"

"Wait 'til I tell Aunt Louise."

"Tell me what?" Aunt Louise suddenly appeared behind him.

"The clerk says they have decided to begin surfacing the *Hunley* this summer," Josh announced.

"That's great news." Aunt Louise started toward the exit. "I hate to leave—I thought we'd have more time. But we don't want to keep Sylvia waiting. We'll come back to the museum another time."

Holding on to his purchase, Josh followed. "Man, this has been some morning. Mom won't believe all I've found out today."

Aunt Louise grinned and gave Josh's hair a toss. "A lot of history—and much more to be found," she said. "By the end of your visit, you'll have a head full."

Chapter 6
THE SIDEWALK CAFE

Josh and Aunt Louise hurried toward Sidewalk Cafe. Mom was already seated at a table reading a medical journal.

Thrusting the shopping bag into Mom's hands, Josh said, in one long breath, "I saw the replica of the *Hunley* submarine. It's something else. And I bought a book about submarines. You won't believe everything I've learned already. Can we come back when they raise the *Hunley?*"

Mom smiled. "I think you'd better slow down, Josh. Sit here by me."

Mom slid the book from the bag and flipped through the pages. "Why, this is a wonderful book. It has lots of pictures of the different submarines, and here are several of the *H. L. Hunley.*"

"The museum guide recommended the book," Aunt Louise said. "It will give Josh more information on the importance of the *Hunley* submarine. The clerk said the vessel will be raised from the ocean floor sooner than first planned."

"I've been following the progress of its recovery on the news," Mom replied.

"I had no idea you liked history until Aunt Louise told me," Josh blurted.

Mom patted Josh on the shoulder. "There are lots of things you don't know about your mom. If I take the new job, I'll have more free time so you can find them out."

Josh's eyes grew wide with surprise. "New job? What new job?"

"After my presentation this morning, I was asked to come to work at the medical center here in Charleston. How about that?"

Josh couldn't believe his ears. "You mean we would live here, in the heart of history?"

"Yes, we'd live in Charleston, right in the lap of history. Aunt Louise can live with us—that is, if she'd like." Mom smiled at Aunt Louise.

"Did you know about this job, Aunt Louise?" Josh asked.

Aunt Louise nodded. "Why do you think we planned this trip?" she asked, winking at Sylvia.

"Cool!" Josh yelled. "I think we should celebrate."

"We can celebrate by eating. I'm starving," Aunt Louise said. "What do you want for lunch, Josh?"

A big grin spread across Josh's face. "A submarine sandwich, what else?" he snickered.

"A great maritime lunch," Aunt Louise said. "I'll have one, too.

"Make it three," beamed Mom.

Chapter 7
THE *HUNLEY* MUSEUM

During lunch, Josh filled Mom in on the events of the morning.

"You definitely have the *Hunley* on the brain," she said. "I guess I was just as excited about it when I was your age."

Turning to Aunt Louise, she asked, "Do you remember taking me to the *Hunley* Museum one summer when I visited in Charleston? I was about Josh's age. Does that place still exist?"

"The *Hunley* Museum? . . . Hmm. That was a long time ago, Sylvia. Let me think." Aunt Louise rubbed her chin, deep in thought. "Yes, I remember now. It was located in the basement of the Citizens and Southern National Bank building at 50 Broad Street. That was the summer of 1967. It didn't stay open very long. It closed in 1969."

"What do you remember about it, Mom?" Josh asked.

With a glint in her eyes Josh had never seen before, she said, "I remember it like it was yesterday. The replica had been recently built and was housed there at the time. The hatches were open and mannequins, dressed as sailors, were seated as crew members. There was one single candle on a makeshift stand. It looked like a great adventure to me. I imagined that I was sailing with the crew."

Mom paused, then continued, "It was years later I heard the *Hunley* referred to as 'the coffin boat.'"

"We read that in the brochure, didn't we, Aunt Louise? And they called it a deathtrap in the video. What else was in the *Hunley* Museum, Mom?"

"Let's see," Mom said. "There was a small-scale *Hunley* displayed on a contour map."

"Were there real pictures of the *Hunley*?" Josh questioned.

"Not many, but there were maps showing where the vessel was last sighted. The thing I remember most was a diorama that included the *Hunley*, with miniature sailors standing around it. I thought it was neat. In another glass case an old rustic revolver and a knife were dis-

The
Hunley Museum
a branch of the Charleston Museum

Painting by Conrad Wise Chapman

Confederate States Submarine
H. L. Hunley
Full scale replica on display at
50 Broad Street.
A gift to the Charleston Museum for the
People of South Carolina from
The Citizens & Southern National Bank
of South Carolina.
Open to the public—No admission charge.

Hunley Museum brochure, courtesy of The Charleston Museum

played. Oh, yes, and there were other miniature boat models. There was the *Housatonic* and the torpedo boat *David*."

"My, Sylvia, you took in a lot to have been so young," Aunt Louise said in surprise.

"I wonder who the knife and revolver belonged to," Josh said.

"I doubt if anybody knew," Mom replied.

"Those items sound like the very same ones the guide at the Charleston Museum told me about this morning," Aunt Louise said. "If they are, they're to be put on display in the new building with the *Hunley* submarine."

"And if we move to Charleston, we can see all those things and the *Hunley* too," Mom added.

Josh looked at Mom and then at Aunt Louise. "If I'm hearing right, Mom's caught the fever."

"It is highly contagious," Aunt Louise smirked.

"Three history buffs in one house. That should be fun." Josh's laughter filled the small cafe.

Mom picked up the check and said softly, "The three history buffs must be on their way."

Chapter 8
FURTHER EXPLORATION

As they headed for the car, Josh asked, "Say, Aunt Louise, since you know so much about Charleston, do you know where Magnolia Cemetery is?"

"Sure. I used to pass its entrance everyday going to work. That's where your Great-great-great-grandfather Cooper is buried. He died during the Civil War. His grave is in the Confederate memorial section."

"My great-great-great-grandfather," sputtered Josh. "That's a lot of *greats*! Is he buried near the *Hunley* crew?"

"Not very," Aunt Louise replied. "Horace Hunley's crew is buried on the Cooper River side of the cemetery. The Confederate memorial section is nearer the entrance."

"Can we go to the cemetery, Mom, please?" Josh

pleaded.

"If it's okay with Aunt Louise, we can. I'd like to visit Grandpa Cooper's grave and see for myself where the *Hunley* crew is buried. ... That is, if Aunt Louise will be our guide."

"Sure," Aunt Louise said. "It's been a long time since I've been there. You drive, Sylvia; I'll give directions."

As they climbed into Mom's car, Aunt Louise said, "You know, they say there's a ghost of an old sea captain who watches over the grave of the *Hunley* crew."

"Really?" Josh shrieked. "I hope we see him."

Mom steered the car up Meeting Street toward the neck of the Charleston peninsula.

Aunt Louise continued, "Come to think of it, I believe we can see the graves of the five members of the *Hunley*'s first crew. Remember the men that died in the first training accident in 1863 and were buried in the mariner's cemetery? That cemetery was located where the Citadel's Hagood Stadium stands today."

"That's what we saw in the video, isn't it?" Josh asked.

"That's right. But from what I've read, the bodies have been moved since the video was made. The remains were recovered last summer during an archeological dig. Several of the bodies were dismembered. Having drowned, their bodies stayed underwater for days before they were recovered. It is thought the bodies had to be cut in order to remove them from the submarine."

"Gross!" Josh shuddered. "That gives me goose bumps."

"The crew members were young Irish immigrants," Aunt Louise continued. "One is said to have been only thirteen years old—not much older than you, Josh. Their bodies were recently buried in Magnolia Cemetery, if I remember correctly."

"Did they put them in the same burial plot with Horace Hunley and his crew?" Josh asked. "I wonder where they'll bury the sailors that are still in the *Hunley?*"

"I really don't know," Aunt Louise answered. "We'll have to ask when we get to the cemetery."

Chapter 9
MAGNOLIA CEMETERY

"There it is! There it is!" shouted Josh. "That sign says Magnolia Cemetery."

"You're right, Josh. I was about to miss it," Aunt Louise said. "Things have grown up around here since I worked at the navy yard."

Mom turned right, through the entrance gate, and followed the drive. She parked in front of an aged white house that served as the office.

Josh unbuckled his seatbelt, opened the door, and jumped out. "Wow, what a big cemetery! And just look at that huge lake. This is the biggest cemetery I've ever seen."

"Yes, it is large," Aunt Louise agreed, "and very old too. It covers 132 acres and dates back to 1849. One could easily get lost here."

"I bet there's more than one ghost in this place," Josh said, forcing his voice to quiver.

MAGNOLIA CEMETERY

ESTABLISHED 1849

"Probably so," said Mom, "but I hope they wait until midnight to come around."

"Mom's a scaredy-cat. Mom's a scaredy-cat," Josh chanted as he ran toward a marble grave marker shaped like a coffin. "That person died in 1853. Isn't that a weird tombstone?"

"There are many interesting grave markers and monuments here at Magnolia," Aunt Louise said. "We could spend hours in here looking at headstones, but let's go find what we've come to see."

Aunt Louise scratched her head. "I know where the Confederate graves are, but I need to ask about the *Hunley* crews. Wait here, I'll be right back." She walked into the office to ask directions.

Josh couldn't be still. He ran among the many graves while Mom read inscriptions on rustic gravestones.

Aunt Louise was soon back, smiling from ear to ear. And she had papers in her hand.

"We're in luck," she said. "The bodies of the Confederate Irish sailors *are* buried here. They're in the same plot with Horace Hunley's crew. That's over near the marsh. The reinterment of the sailors' bodies was only last month. The lady in the office was excited that we knew it. She said I was one of the first tourists who had asked to see the graves. This program tells about the recent burial ceremony. She said it was a great tribute to the five courageous patriots."

"I like that," said Josh. "Five courageous patriots. ... They should also be remembered as pioneers."

"I'm sure they will be," Mom said. "Pioneers who died for a cause they believed in and for a technology yet to be realized."

"Josh and I were talking about that at the museum this morning," Aunt Louise said. "We have the modern-day submarines because of brave individuals like those young Irish sailors. Their fatal accident led to a quantum leap in naval warfare."

"What are we waiting for?" Josh asked. "Let's go find their graves. How do we get there?"

Aunt Louise unfolded the papers in her hand.

"Here's a map of the cemetery." Pointing, she said, "There's King Circle. The *Hunley* plot is on that road. It's a good walk from here. The Confederate section is there, to the right of the office. Why don't we go there first?"

"Lead on," Mom said.

Chapter 10
GRANDPA COOPER

Mom and Josh followed Aunt Louise along a path between gravestones until they came to the Confederate section. They stood in silence, gazing at the tall monument and row after row of small white headstones,

each representing a man who died for the Confederacy. A small flag graced each grave.

"This is a grand memorial to our Confederate dead," Aunt Louise said. "I had forgotten how massive and impressive it is. I hope I can find Great-grandfather's grave."

She walked past the tall monument, looking down at headstones. Josh and Mom followed.

Josh tried counting the headstones, but there were so many he kept losing count. He continued to follow Aunt Louise as she tromped through the field of white stones. Finally, at the tenth row, she stopped. Bending

down, she looked closely at a marker.

"Cooper. S. J. Cooper," she read. "This is your great-great-great-grandfather's grave. He died in Charleston during the Civil War.

"Did he get shot?" Josh asked.

"No. Grandmother told me he died of a fever in a camp hospital."

"He was still a hero," Josh said. "He gave his life for a cause."

"That's an amiable thought," Mom said. "He *did* die for a cause, just as all of these men did."

"What else do you know about Grandpa Cooper, Aunt Louise?" Josh asked.

"The S stands for Samuel. My great-grandmother was named after him. She was called Sam."

"I think that's in our family's genealogy book," Mom said. "We'll look it up when we get home."

"Are we related to Lord Ashley Cooper?" Josh asked.

"I'm afraid not, Josh. Samuel's family lived in the Upstate not far from us, near Greenville," replied Aunt Louise. "However, the name Cooper is pronounced the same."

Josh began to read the names on other tombstones. "Do we have any more relatives buried here?" he asked.

"No, just Grandpa Samuel. My other great-grandfather survived the war and lived to be ninety," Aunt Louise added. "He was from the Upstate too."

She turned from Grandpa's grave and said, "Now, Josh, let's go find the *Hunley* plot."

Josh gave a military salute and said, "Yes, Ma'am, lead the way. I'm ready to march."

Chapter 11
THE GRAVES OF
THE *HUNLEY* CREWS

Leaving the Confederate section behind, they walked briskly in the direction of the river. A cool breeze carried the salty aroma of the sea up from the marsh. Mom and Aunt Louise chatted as Josh hurried on ahead.

"This is King's Circle," Josh called back, "but there are so many graves!"

"The lady in the office said there is a palmetto palm planted at the back of the plot, beside a monument," Aunt Louise offered. "The graves are situated on a knoll."

"Oh, there it is!" Josh pointed to the other side of the circle. "I see the tree and the marker. And there's a short wall around it."

Josh ran to the plot. "I see some headstones," he yelled. Mom and Aunt Louise moved quickly to catch up.

Standing near the edge of the plot, they silently read the names of the second crew and the date of death carved on the monument. A tombstone marked the grave of Horace L. Hunley; another marked the grave of crewman Thomas W. Parks. The graves of the remaining six crew members were denoted only by small marble stones, each bearing a number and the initials of the dead. A withered wreath adorned the back of the plot.

"Where are the Irish sailors' graves?" Josh questioned. "Aren't they supposed to be here?"

"They're at the back, where the faded wreath stands," Aunt Louise answered. "Look closely—you can see the fresh dirt under the pine straw. The lady in the office said a monument will soon be erected with the sailors' names. She also said that the sailors still in the *Hunley* will be buried in this same plot".

"They should put up one big monument in memory of all these amazing men," Mom remarked.

"They gave their lives for maritime history, didn't they?" Josh asked thoughtfully.

"Yes. They are some of America's unsung heroes," Aunt Louise replied. "With the reinterment of the Irish boys and the burial of the crew members still in the sub, perhaps they will finally receive the credit they deserve."

"Rightly so," added Mom. "Rightly so!"

Chapter 12
THE GHOST

Josh began to poke around the edge of the plot.

"What are you doing?" Mom asked.

"Looking for the ghost of the old sea captain. I'm sure he's here."

Aunt Louise smiled. "You may be right. My friend Buddy, the tugboat captain, told me the story of the ghost seen near Horace Hunley's grave."

Josh's eyes

brightened. "Tell me, tell me!" he shouted.

Aunt Louise sat down at the edge of the plot. "It all began in August 1863," she said, "when the *Hunley* was brought to Charleston. Seems that each time the submarine began a mission, an old man dressed in a sea captain's uniform was seen standing near the dock. His hair and beard were as white as snow. His leathered face bore the wrinkles of time. As the vessel pushed out to sea, the old sea captain would wave his hat and shout, 'Bon Voyage!'

"He was seen the day of the first accident, when the Irish sailors drowned. And he was there at Fort Johnson the day Horace Hunley took his crew out and never returned. He was reported to have been there February 17, 1864, the eve Dixon and his crew left Sullivan's Island. No one knew his name or where he came from. It was not known when or where he had served as a ship's captain. But his actions showed maritime pride. He was always there to convey good luck to the sailors of the *Hunley*.

"After the third accident, the old sea captain was seemingly forgotten. It wasn't until the winter of 1871 that he was seen again, this time as a ghost at Horace Hunley's grave. It was on a full-moon night that the sea captain's ghost first appeared in the cemetery.

"Though it was winter, the weather was nice, and
the groundskeeper and his wife were enjoying a walk

through the cemetery. They headed toward the Cooper River, knowing the water would be shimmering in the moonlight. As they neared the *Hunley* plot, suddenly a hazy mass, like a small isolated cloud, floated toward them. The wife became frightened, but her husband assured her it was only fog creeping up from the river.

"As they drew closer to the grave, the old sea captain, with hat in hand, appeared, kneeling at the grave. The footsteps of the couple broke the silence and the captain disappeared right before their eyes.

"Since that night, he has been seen many times at the grave, always kneeling. But when people get near, he disappears into thin air."

"Cool story!" Josh exclaimed. "Is it true?"

"That's the way it was told to me," laughed Aunt Louise. "Since I left Charleston, I haven't heard any reports of the sea captain's visits. But, with all the commotion now about the *Hunley*, who knows? Anything can happen."

"It can happen after we get out of here," Mom said, as she headed toward the car.

"I told you Mom was a scaredy-cat," Josh teased. "We'll have to bring her here again when there's a full moon. That will really scare her."

"I'm afraid not, Josh. The gates close at six o'clock,"

Aunt Louise said.

"Shucks." Josh let out a little moan. "It would be great to see a real ghost."

"Maybe for you, but not for me," said Mom. "Let's get out of here, now!"

Josh laughed all the way to the car.

"He sure has enjoyed today," Mom told Aunt Louise, "and so have I."

"You're going to love living in Charleston, Sylvia," Aunt Louise said. "I can't wait to move back. We'll have such fun together."

As Mom unlocked the car door, Josh called to Aunt Louise. "Hey, let Mom chauffeur."

Aunt Louise chuckled as she climbed into the back seat after Josh.

Riding back to the hotel, Josh talked non-stop about his first day in the historic port city. "Where will we begin tomorrow's tour, Mom?"

"I'd like to start at White Point Gardens on the Battery. We can see the memorial to the *Hunley* crew there

. . . and a tree where pirates were hanged."

"Pirates in Charleston?" Josh became so excited he almost came out of his seat.

"Yep! Pirates in Charleston," Mom answered. "But pirates will have to wait. We've had enough history for one day. Don't you agree?"

"Yes, ma'am. Enough for one day."

Josh turned to look at Aunt Louise. Her eyes seemed bigger than ever—not just because of her thick glasses but from all the excitement of the day. Aunt Louise gave Josh a wink. They both smiled and Josh leaned a little closer to his favorite aunt. Maybe he was getting too big to snuggle, but it would be okay just for today.

Aunt Louise put her arm around Josh and he could feel the warmth of her arm on his cool face. He felt warm inside too. This had been a wonderful day, and tomorrow three history buffs would enjoy more exciting sites in the historical city called Charleston.

Chapter 13
A RAINY DAY

Josh opened his eyes to the sound of rain tapping softly on glass. He jumped out of bed and ran to the window.

"Oh, no," he mumbled, "a rainy day in Charleston! What do we do now?"

His voice woke Aunt Louise. Rolling over to face the window, she said, "So it's raining. We'll just have to make the best of it, Josh. A little rain won't hurt us."

"But I wanted to go to Fort Sumter, and Mom wants to go to White Point Gardens."

Aunt Louise sat up and reached for her glasses. "So we'll change our plans. We can go to Fort Moultrie—they've got a great visitors center—or to the Old Exchange Building. There's much history in both places. We could go back to the Charleston Museum."

"I suppose so," Josh said, disappointed.

"I believe there's more information about the *Hunley* at Fort Moultrie," Aunt Louise said, trying to give Josh's spirits a boost. "I remember reading it somewhere—just can't remember where. And they have a short movie on the history of Fort Moultrie for tourists to see. You'll enjoy that. Or, we can tour the old fort—it might not be raining there."

By this time their conversation had awakened Mom.

Sitting up in bed, she said, "Sounds like we'll have a great day in spite of the rain. But remember, we don't have to see everything today. When we move to Charleston, these things will still be here."

"I can't believe we are really moving to Charleston." Josh's mood lightened suddenly at that thought. "Where will we live?"

"Good question," Mom answered. "I'll have to begin my job the first of next month, but I want you to stay in Union until school is out. Since Aunt Louise will be moving here with us, maybe you could stay with her until June. How about it, Aunt Louise?"

"You must have been reading my mind, Sylvia. Last night in bed, I came up with almost the same plan. The lease on my apartment is up the first of May, so I can move into your house and stay with Josh until the house is sold."

"I can't believe how things are falling into place," Mom said. "I'll put my house on the market next week. Hopefully it will sell by July. I'll take an apartment here in the city and be on the lookout for a house near a school. How does that sound to you, Josh?"

"Great!" Josh answered. "I'll miss my friends at home, but I can't wait to move to Charleston."

Mom looked at her watch. "It's already nine o'clock. Let's get dressed and go down to breakfast before the dining room closes. We'll discuss our plans later."

They were all dressed and ready to go out the door when the telephone rang. Mom reached for the receiver.

"Yes, this is she. ... Of course. What time? ... I'll be there. Thank you for calling." She smiled a half smile as she hung up the phone. "I'm afraid you two will have to tour by yourselves for the second day. That call was from the medical center and they want me there by ten o'clock to sign papers and get information concerning my new position. Do you mind, Aunt Louise?"

"Of course not," Aunt Louise replied. "Your job is of first importance. Josh and I can take care of ourselves."

"Sure we can," agreed Josh. "We can find lots to do when we're together. Come on, I'm hungry."

"Me too," Aunt Louise added. "Breakfast is waiting."

Chapter 14
FORT MOULTRIE

Mom rushed through her meal and took a cab to the medical center. Aunt Louise and Josh finished their cereal, then headed for the hotel's parking garage, carrying their umbrellas.

Unlocking the car door Aunt Louise said, "Let's go to Fort Moultrie first. Then we can come back to the Old Exchange Building after lunch."

"Whatever you say. You're the leader when it comes to Charleston." Josh buckled his seatbelt, then asked, "Where is Fort Moultrie?"

"It's on Sullivan's Island, across the Cooper River. You'll get to go over the tall Cooper River bridges. Remember, we saw them from Magnolia Cemetery. They're the tallest bridges in South Carolina. It took me a long time to learn to drive over them, especially the old one. Now with the one-way traffic, I don't mind so much."

Aunt Louise drove up Meeting Street, past the museum.

"This is the same street we took to Magnolia Cemetery, isn't it?" asked Josh.

"It surely is, but we'll take Highway 17 North to get to the islands. It turns off before the cemetery. That will take us into the town of Mount Pleasant. From Mount Pleasant we'll cross the creek to Sullivan's Island."

Aunt Louise exited at Highway 17 and began the climb onto the Cooper River Bridge.

"Whoa!" cried Josh. "You said the bridges were tall, but I didn't know they were this tall. Look! I see ships down there. They look small from way up here. What's that big ship over on the far bank?"

Glancing quickly to the right, Aunt Louise replied. "That's the USS *Yorktown*. It's an aircraft carrier used in World War II. It's open to the public as a museum. We'll go there one day."

"More and more history," said Josh. "Do you think we can ever see it all?"

Aunt Louise laughed. "No, not really, but we'll try."

As they exited the bridge and drove onto Coleman Boulevard, the rain stopped.

"That's Charleston for you. It doesn't always rain over the whole city at one time. We'll still need our umbrellas though. It may rain again at any time."

Josh was quiet as Aunt Louise drove onto Sullivan's Island. He was enthralled with the marshland. It looked so different from the Upstate—palmetto trees, oleander bushes, and tall grasses were everywhere. What a thrill to be going onto an island! Seeing all the houses and condominiums along the marsh, he exclaimed, "I thought Fort Moultrie would be on a deserted island."

"Afraid not," Aunt Louise replied. "It's been hundreds of years since this island was deserted. It's now crowded with the homes of year-round residents and rental property for tourists. It has nice beaches. Look there, you can see the island lighthouse."

"Wow! A real lighthouse! It doesn't look like most lighthouses."

"I guess there aren't many square lighthouses," Aunt Louise responded. "It was built in 1962 to replace the Morris Island Lighthouse. It even has an elevator."

"Can we go in it?" Josh asked.

"No, it's maintained by the U. S. Coast Guard. For safety reasons, the public isn't allowed. Fort Moultrie is right ahead. See the signs. The fort is there on the left side of the street. The visitors center is that brick building on the right. That's where the movie will be. We'll park behind the building. If it starts raining again, we won't have far to walk."

Chapter 15
ANOTHER *HUNLEY*

Josh was out of his seatbelt and on the sidewalk in a flash.

"Hey, wait for me," Aunt Louise called as she locked the car doors.

She followed Josh up the steps to the back entrance

of the building. Small drops of rain fell from the eaves, and Aunt Louise was glad they had their umbrellas.

Josh pushed open the glass door leading into the building, then stopped in his tracks. He couldn't believe his eyes. There in the middle of the lobby was a replica of the *Hunley* submarine. It was similar to the replica at the Charleston Museum, but he could see inside it. One end had been cut off.

Before Aunt Louise could say a word Josh ducked under the velvet rope and was seated in the first hand-crank position. He began to turn the crank just as Aunt Louise approached.

"Look, another *Hunley*," he cried, "and this one I can get inside."

"Yes, another *Hunley*, but I don't think you're supposed to be inside. The velvet rope is there to discourage people from entering. Come out and we'll ask someone about this replica."

Josh frowned, but he climbed out of the replica and followed Aunt Louise to the information desk where a park ranger was assisting a tourist. As they waited, Josh asked, "Where did this *Hunley* come from?"

"We'll have to ask the ranger," Aunt Louise replied. "I'm sure she knows."

The tourist thanked the ranger and turned to leave.

The young woman behind the desk smiled at Aunt Louise and said, "I'm Dawn, your park ranger. May I help you? I see this young man is interested in the *Hunley*."

"He certainly is," Aunt Louise answered. "He was wondering where this replica came from."

"Are you familiar with the history of the *Hunley* submarine?" she asked.

Aunt Louise laughed, "Yes, we are well acquainted with the history of the submarine, but we didn't know there was more than one replica in Charleston."

"Did you see the movie *The Hunley*?" Dawn asked.

"No. Only yesterday did we hear the movie had been made. I do hope we can see it in the near future."

Guiding them toward the replica, the ranger said, "You're in luck. This is a full-scale replica of the *H. L. Hunley* submarine built by Turner Network Television for the movie. It's on loan to us for the month. As you see, the end of the vessel is open so the actors could get in for the filming of the movie. You can see the eight cranking stations used to propel it."

"We learned about that in the brochure, didn't we, Aunt Louise?" Josh remarked.

"That's right," Aunt Louise said, placing her hand gently on Josh's head, "but let's listen to what the ranger has to say. We can learn more."

Dawn continued, "There were nine members of the crew. Eight worked the cranks to propel the vessel, and the ninth acted as captain."

"Was that Lieutenant George Dixon?" Josh asked.

"Why, yes. You do know the history of the *Hunley*," exclaimed Ranger Dawn. "I guess you also know the story about the gold coin Dixon carried in his pocket."

Josh shook his head no.

"I may have heard it, but I can't recall," Aunt Louise said.

"At the beginning of the Civil War," the ranger began, "Lieutenant George Dixon was engaged to a longtime sweetheart, Miss Queenie Bennett, from Mobile, Alabama."

"Yuck! A sweetheart," groaned Josh, rolling his eyes.

"Yes, a very beautiful one," Ranger Dawn continued, winking at Aunt Louise. "Their romance had blossomed into its second year, and they vowed to be married when the war was over. It is recorded that Queenie gave her sweetheart a twenty-dollar gold piece for good luck as he departed with the army to fight.

"Not long after, in the battle of Shiloh, Dixon was hit in the thigh by a bullet. The shot would have killed him had it not first struck the gold piece in his pocket, which pierced his flesh. When the coin was removed, it was in the shape of a bell, with the bullet firmly imbedded in the gold. History tells us that Dixon highly prized the good-luck piece, even in its mangled condition, and always carried it in his pocket."

"I bet it was in his pocket when he boarded the *Hunley*," Josh added.

"Historians think so," Dawn agreed. "It will probably be found in the bottom of the vessel when it is brought to the surface."

"That's something I'd like to see!" Josh exclaimed.

Aunt Louise nodded in agreement and said, "Thanks for the story. The more we look, the more we see and hear about the *Hunley*. There seems to be no end to the history."

"You're right," Ranger Dawn replied. "More historical facts about this great submarine are emerging everyday. There'll be even more when it is raised. Do you know about the mobile exhibit that's touring America? It offers a unique hands-on history of the submarine. The exhibit is housed in the trailer of an eighteen wheeler. It's owned by Friends of the *Hunley*. Right now, it's at a Confederate celebration in Virginia. But it's on display here from time to time."

"Just what is in the exhibit?" Aunt Louise asked.

"A forty-two-foot model of the *Hunley* is the focal point of the exhibit. It's the first thing you see as you board the display, at the sub's rear by the propeller.

"You follow a wooden boardwalk down the length of the vessel, so you get a good look at the solid construction and smooth design. The design will amaze you. The sub's canoe-like shape allowed it to pass through water like a fish. The model is mounted on wooden blocks affixed to the boardwalk and it rests on its starboard side. It is in this same position the real *Hunley* has rested for the past 136 years on the ocean floor.

"A rustic image of George Dixon meets you at the bow of the vessel. You might be surprised at how young a man he was to serve as captain of the *H. L. Hunley*. A model of the torpedo used to sink the *Housatonic* is displayed below the photograph of Captain Dixon.

"The most dramatic element of the exhibit stands at the end of the boardwalk. A cross section of the submarine shows the cramped quarters inside."

"Sort of like this one?" Josh asked pointing to the replica in the lobby.

"Yes, but not as much of the vessel. You can see the simple hand crank and the harsh conditions crew members endured. Friends of the *Hunley* makes the exhibit available to schools, festivals, and other events. It's a very impressive exhibit for people of all ages."

"I'm going to tell Miss Adams about it," Josh proclaimed. "Maybe it can come to our school."

"That's a great idea," Aunt Louise said.

"May I climb in, Ranger Dawn?" Josh asked.

"Sure. The velvet ribbon is there to keep unguided tourists out."

Josh climbed in and pretended to propel the vessel.

"Is today's movie about the *Hunley*?" Aunt Louise asked.

"No, it tells the history of Fort Moultrie and the wars in which it has been used. I think you two will like it."

"And, I can rest my weary feet," Aunt Louise laughed. "Thank you for sharing this wonderful information with us." Turning to Josh she said, "Want to see the movie? It's about to begin."

Chapter 16
REST FOR THE WEARY

Josh followed Aunt Louise into the theater and they took seats in the dark. Aunt Louise closed her eyes and was soon fast asleep.

Josh was fascinated by the battle scenes portrayed in the movie, but his mind kept wandering. He couldn't stop thinking about the *Hunley*—and about moving to Charleston. It was a lot to absorb.

When the film was over and the lights came on, Josh laughed and poked Aunt Louise. "Wake up, sleepyhead. You've missed the whole movie."

Squinting her eyes against the light, Aunt Louise sat up straight. "Well, that gives us a reason to come again."

Back in the lobby, Josh was disappointed to see that the weather had grown worse. "It's pouring rain," he whined. "It's raining so hard you can't see Fort Moultrie."

"Well, we could watch the movie again," Aunt Louise suggested.

"Or, for the first time," giggled Josh.

Just then, the cellular phone in Aunt Louise's purse rang.

"That's probably your mom, Josh. She said she would call when she was free. Hello. . . . I figured it was you. How was your morning? . . . Really? That's nice. Yes, we're in the park building at Fort Moultrie. It's raining very hard. . . . Yes, we had planned to tour the fort, but if it keeps raining like this, we'll probably wait until another time. . . . Say that again. . . . They already have a place you can stay until we can move? . . . That was quick."

Josh tugged on Aunt Louise's jacket sleeve. "What is she saying? What is she saying?"

"Yes, we can do that. We'll see you as soon as we can. You did say Ashley Avenue? . . . Yes, I know. Bye now."

"What? What? What did Mom say? What does she want us to do?"

"Hold your horses, Josh." Aunt Louise returned her phone to her purse. "The medical center has already found your mom an apartment, on Ashley Avenue. Seems that one of the instructors needed a roommate and has invited Sylvia to move in. She'll live there until we can move to Charleston. It's downtown and very close to her work. Ashley Avenue is an old, historical street. It's a nice area to live. She wants us to meet her at Colonial Lake, on Ashley Avenue. We'll take a look at her new *home* and then we'll go to lunch."

Aunt Louise handed Josh an umbrella as they stepped through the glass door at the back entrance. "Like I said, you never can tell where in Charleston it's going to rain. I'll bet it's dry downtown."

Stooped beneath their open umbrellas, they hurried to the car. Aunt Louise called, "Rain or no rain, there's lots to see and do in old 'Charles Town.'"

PART II

Chapter 17
AUNT LOUISE MOVES IN
May 1, 2000

Life had been hectic for Josh, Mom, and Aunt Louise since the trip to Charleston in April. Aunt Louise emptied her apartment and moved in with Josh. Mom put the house up for sale and settled into her apartment in Charleston.

Josh told Ms. Adams and his classmates all about the CSS *Hunley* submarine. Ms. Adams designated a section of the bulletin board for a display on the *Hunley*. The class began bringing newspaper articles about the submarine to school.

The guest bedroom at Josh's house was filled with Aunt Louise's books, photograph albums, trunks, baskets, hat boxes, and plastic crates of memorabilia. Trying to sort through her treasured things, Aunt Louise found it difficult to decide what to discard and what to keep for the move to Charleston.

While rummaging through a box of photographs, she came across pictures taken in Charleston the summer Sylvia was nine. "Look, Josh. Here's a photo of your mom at Fort Sumter."

"Hey," Josh exclaimed, "she's riding the cannon like a horse!"

Other pictures documented the family's trip to the *Hunley* Museum. One photo showed the entrance on Broad Street. And to Aunt Louise's great joy, there was a picture of the newly built replica of the *Hunley*, mannequins and all. Handing it to Josh, she said, "These are not just *my* memories, but your Mom's too. Put them with *your* cherished things. They are family history now."

"Thanks. I'll put them in my special box under the bed. But first I want to take them to school and share them with my class."

Sylvia liked her new job and her roommate, Ruth. She spent her free time house hunting, which gave her the chance to learn her way around Charleston. She kept in touch with Josh and Aunt Louise by phone and e-mail, and she drove home on weekends. Articles on the raising of the *Hunley* appeared daily in the local newspaper, and sending the news to Josh was a daily task. Arriving at her office early she would hurriedly send an email bringing him up to date. She followed the column called "The *Hunley* Project" in the *Post & Courier* and clipped articles to take to Josh on weekends.

 May 7
Dear Josh,
In today's paper there was a great story about the *Hunley* with a picture. The headline read, "Sub's final journey to begin this friday." The article covered the entire history of the vessel. Sounds as if the *Hunley* is really coming home! A good article. I'll save it for you.
Love, Mom

 May 8
Dear Josh,
"The *Hunley* Project" reports that a hole about the size of a grapefruit was found in the forward conning tower of the sub. It is thought the damage may have been from a projectile during the attack on the *Housatonic*.
Love, Mom

May 12
Hey, Josh.
Exciting news! Today's headline reads "*Hunley* recovery begins." My co-workers are as thrilled as you are—everyone is talking about the *Hunley*. Gotta run. Mom

May 15
Dear Josh,
Post & Courier's headline reads "*Hunley* site excavation starts today." The article says, "Divers will vacuum sand around the Confederate submarine *H.L. Hunley* this morning as they excavate the underwater battlefield looking for artifacts. . . . Divers will begin dredging a trough around the *Hunley* looking for clues and pieces of the sub that might have fallen in the February 1864 attack on the USS *Housatonic*."
Love, Mom

May 17
Dear Josh,
Things seem to be moving fast. Archaeologists have recovered the two conning towers and have dug down to the top of the sub. Small sections of the bow and stern can be seen, but most of the vessel is still hidden by the sandy ocean bottom. Sounds like it won't be long now. I'm

still looking for a house.
Love you. Mom

May 23
Dear Josh,
Today's report said the *Hunley's* rudder is broken off and missing. It is also reported that the fore and aft sections are much more knife-like than previously thought. The ends are made of cast iron and are weaker than the rest of the hull, which was formed from a locomotive boiler. How's the school bulletin board coming? See you Friday. Tell Aunt Louise to call me.
Over and out. Mom

May 25
Dear Josh,
Divers have located an object that might be the missing rudder. Saw a house last night I liked. Will tour after work today. Tell you about it when I get home.
Love you. Mom

May 26
No new *Hunley* news today. I liked the house. It's on James Island, not far from work and near a school. See you tonight.
Mom

Sylvia was glad to be home for the weekend. She and Aunt Louise spent time showing the house. The news articles were brought for Josh. He spent much time clipping the articles from the paper. After sharing them with his class he would give them to Aunt Louise for her *Hunley* scrapbook.

May 29
Dear Josh,
The weekend was great. I hope it won't be long until we are all together in a new house. About the *Hunley* . . . the local news this weekend reported that the spar has been discovered, still attached to the vessel. The spar is made of iron, not wood as first thought. It is bolted on at the sub's bow, near the bottom—not directly on top as depicted on the *Hunley* model you saw outside the Charleston Museum. This is going to be a busy week at work. My email may be scarce.
Mom

June 2
Dear Josh,
"The *Hunley* Project" reports that molds are being taken of the submarine's hull. Using fiberglass tape, the divers wrapped sections of the sunken vessel to create a mold that will show

the sub's curvature. According to the newspaper, about half of the sub's top section has been exposed. Once a section is investigated, it is quickly covered with a layer of sandbags for protection.

Gotta go. Mom

When Sylvia got home late Friday, Aunt Louise greeted her with the news that a couple liked the house and would be back on Sunday to talk business.

As Sylvia drove back to Charleston Sunday evening, she felt lighthearted. A contract had been signed on the Union house and the sale would be final by the first of July. The three history buffs would be together again soon under the same roof.

Ruth had saved the weekend newspapers. "Hunley lift date moved up," one headline read.

 June 6

Exciting news! The *Hunley* will be brought up in early August. If all goes well, we will be here together for the event. I'm going to look at the house on James Island again this evening. I think it's the one for us.

Love, Mom

June 7
Dear Josh,
The *Hunley* raising is on hold as the crane they're using for the excavation isn't strong enough. The hunt for a larger one may take several weeks. Let's hope not. I signed a contract on the James Island house. I spoke with Aunt Louise. She's bringing you to Charleston Saturday so we can all take a look.
Love, Mom

Chapter 18
THE NEW HOUSE

Josh and Aunt Louise arrived at Sylvia's apartment at ten o'clock Saturday morning. Sylvia was just cooking breakfast: pancakes, Josh's favorite. Ruth was out of town for the weekend, so the three had the apartment to themselves.

Josh's tongue moved fifty miles an hour telling Mom about everything, barely allowing the others speak. Mom finally sent him out to the side yard to see the fishpond so she and Aunt Louise could talk.

"You're going to like the house. It has a sewing room, just for you. There is also a large backyard with trees for Josh to climb."

"What did you say about me?" Josh questioned, coming through the door.

"I was telling Aunt Louise that I think you both will

like the house on James Island. As soon as I clean up here and get dressed, we'll go see it."

"Does it have a swimming pool?"

"Afraid not, Josh, but there is a community pool where you can swim. And we'll be only five miles from the beach."

"All right!"

Sylvia's apartment was on the first floor of an old Charleston single house. A narrow porch ran the length of the house, facing the courtyard. A wrought iron fence encircled the small yard, which contained flowerbeds and a fishpond. The front door was on the side of the house facing the street. Upstairs was a second apartment where a young couple lived. The third-floor apartment was vacant.

"There's nothing more charming than a Charleston single house," Aunt Louise said. "And the fishpond's fountain gives it historical charm." Her eyes danced. "Oh, it's so good to be back in Charleston!"

Soon, Aunt Louise began swatting gnats. "Let's go before the Charleston bugs get us."

"Charleston bugs?" Josh said. "I didn't know Charleston had its own bugs."

Mom laughed. "Get in the car before you find out for sure."

Everyone buckled up and Mom headed for the James Island Connector. Within minutes she was turning into the drive of their new house. Josh and Aunt Louise explored the many rooms and the backyard while Mom talked to the realtor.

As they backed out of the drive an hour later, Mom announced, "We can move in right after I sign the papers on July 1. Why don't we do something special to celebrate. Anyone want to drive out to Folly Beach for lunch?"

"Yeah!" Josh called from the back seat. "You're the best, Mom!"

The little beach town was busy, but Sylvia found a parking space on Center Street, right in front of a small restaurant.

After they ate, the three walked across Arctic Avenue to the ocean. Aunt Louise and Mom strolled along the edge of the water. Josh played keep away with the incoming tide.

He couldn't resist for long and soon ran into the surf. Before he knew it, he was soaking wet.

"That was fun!" he cried, shivering from the coldness of the water.

"Yes the beach is always fun," Mom said. "Next time we'll bring bathing suits and towels!"

The afternoon passed quickly, and in no time, they

were watching the sunset, the sky golden and pink.

"The sunset looks like a sunrise," Josh said.

"Yes, but it won't take you long to find out the difference," Aunt Louise declared.

As the sun disappeared below the horizon, Josh lamented, "Wow, you're right. It's getting dark fast."

Josh, Mom, and Aunt Louise rode back to the peninsula in silence. Josh was fast asleep before they reached the apartment.

As they turned onto Ashley Avenue, Aunt Louise yawned and said, "Another wonderful day in Charleston. But now I'm looking forward to a quick dinner and a wonderful night of sleep."

The following morning, Josh jumped out of bed and rushed to the front porch to get the Sunday paper. Running into the kitchen where Mom was making coffee, he said, "Today, I can find 'The *Hunley* Project' for myself."

Spreading the paper on the table, he began his search for the column.

"Here it is, in the local news section."

"Good. I'm just in time to hear the latest on the Hunley," Aunt Louise said, joining him at the table.

Josh read, "'It is reported that historians are surprised at how the Hunley looks. It is much more sleek and technologically advanced than is recorded in history books.' May I cut this out, Mom?"

"Of course you can. You can take it home with you. That's one I won't have to save. The scissors are in the cabinet drawer."

Josh carefully cut the article from the paper and put it in his sports bag with his clothes. Miss Adams will be glad to have a new article for the bulletin board," he said.

In the afternoon, Aunt Louise and Josh drove back to Union, and Sylvia prepared for the workweek.

 June 14, 2000
Hi, Son.
Am in a hurry this morning. The *Hunley's* spar is lifted from the ocean. Seems a piece broke off as they detached it from the sub. It has been taken to the *Hunley* Conservation Lab for examination. The chairman of the *Hunley* Commission is quoted as saying, "This is history unfolding right here. It is a miracle we found it, much less have it back in this shape. This is a historical moment. It's been 136 years since this vessel touched South Carolina soil."
Love you. Mom

June 16, 2000

Hi, family.

Hunley raising still on hold as they continue the search for a larger crane. Will not be home until tomorrow. Having dinner with friends this evening.

Mom

Early Saturday Sylvia drove home to Union. There was much to do in getting ready to move. Aunt Louise and Josh had already packed many of their personal things. Sylvia still needed to sort through her business files and household belongings. The couple who bought the house wanted to move in as soon as possible, but Sylvia had not yet heard from the contract on the James Island house.

The three were very tired as Sylvia loaded the car to drive back to Charleston Sunday evening.

"I'll be glad when we can all be together," she said, giving Josh a good-bye hug. "Don't let Aunt Louise work too hard."

"And don't forget the *Hunley* news!" shouted Josh, as Sylvia started the car.

"There's no way I can forget the *Hunley*. It's on the mind of every history buff in Charleston."

When Sylvia arrived back at the apartment, there

was a note that the real estate office had called. The house on James Island was hers. The signing was scheduled for Tuesday.

She picked up the phone and called Aunt Louise right away. "Hi. Hope I didn't wake you. Great news! The house on James Island is ours. Tell Josh we'll be moving soon. Isn't that wonderful?"

"Yes, indeed," responded a sleepy Aunt Louise. "I can't believe I'm really moving back to Charleston, my favorite place in the world."

"And it's becoming my favorite, too. See you soon. Good night."

Chapter 19
MOVING DAY

Moving day finally came. Mom had driven home the night before and the three were up, bright and early, waiting for the movers. A breakfast of cold cereal was eaten in haste before the truck arrived. The movers began loading at ten o'clock. By two o'clock, the truck was loaded and so were the two family cars. There was just enough space in Mom's car for Josh to sit.

"Good-bye, old house. I'll miss you," Josh said, as Mom backed out of the driveway. "Take care of the new owners."

"And I know the new owners will take care of the house," Mom added, turning away so Josh couldn't see the tears in her eyes. She was leaving ten years of memories. She quickly reminded herself that a new home and new memories awaited the family in Charleston.

The new house was larger than the old one, with plenty of room for Aunt Louise's treasures and a large yard for her flowers. There was a double garage with a paved driveway, just right for Josh and his skateboard.

No more riding the school bus for Josh. The local school was just around the corner. He could ride his bike.

On his third day in the new house Josh discovered the neighbors had a son, Scott, his age. By the second week they were best friends. Scott was as excited about the *Hunley* raising as Josh. Every morning after Mom left for work, and Aunt Louise finished reading the newspaper, Josh and Scott took turns finding articles about the *Hunley*. They would seek out "The *Hunley* Project" and read it first.

"The *Hunley* Project" kept the boys up to date:

☆ July 21, 2000
New crane arrives in Charleston after a 12,000-mile trip from the Dominican Republic. The recovery project continues.

☆ July 27, 2000
A third hole is found in the submarine—this one, about the size of a small dinner plate, sits low on the starboard bow. Divers also find

strains of rope buried in the silt next to the sub and a mysterious growth on the bow.

☆ July 28, 2000
Divers install four of the lift slings in place.

☆ July 29, 2000
While strapping on the lifting truss, divers discover the *Hunley's* missing snorkels. Project manager Bob Neyland said the two snorkels were lying nearby on the ocean floor. The snorkel set was among the last missing pieces of the submarine. The fact that the snorkels were found near the vessel proves it hadn't moved much since it went down 136 years ago.

☆ July 30, 2000
Divers secure into place six of the thirty-two straps needed to lift the sub. After a strap is placed, foam is added to cushion the vessel and hold it in position. Diving teams work around the clock to get the *Hunley* secured for its ride to the surface and then to the conservation lab in North Charleston. The projected date for the raising is August 8, 2000.

After reading the latest news each morning, the

boys would clip articles and give them to Aunt Louise. The *Hunley* scrapbook was getting thicker by the day.

"It won't be long now," Josh said. "August is here already. Let's do a *Hunley* countdown."

"Great idea," Scott agreed. "We need a calendar."

"No problem. I'll make us one on the computer." In a few minutes, Josh had printed out two calendars, one for each of them.

"That was fast. You'll have to teach me to do that," Scott said.

"Piece of cake!" Josh said proudly.

Scott counted, "1, 2, 3, 4, 5, 6, 7, 8. Only eight days until the *Hunley* comes home."

For the next seven days the boys met and read the latest news on the *Hunley* project, marking off each day on their calendars.

When Scott wasn't around, Josh and Aunt Louise talked about their plans for August 8. Scott's grandfather worked at the U. S. Coast Guard base, so he would be watching from a boat.

Aunt Louise and Mom had decided they would go to Sullivan's Island for viewing. They knew they would have to get there early. Not knowing how long the surfacing would take, they would carry a cooler and lawn chairs, as well as sunscreen and umbrellas.

Chapter 20
THE *HUNLEY* COMES HOME
August 8, 2000

Aunt Louise woke at 4:30. Rubbing her eyes, she sat up, reached for her glasses, and slid her feet into her slippers. In the darkness, she felt her way down the hall to Josh's room. Giving his shoulder a gentle shake, she whispered, "The big day is here. The *Hunley* is coming home."

Josh opened his eyes and jumped up. "I know and I'm ready to go. See, I dressed last night."

Aunt Louise laughed. Sure enough, Josh was fully dressed except for his shoes.

"So you are. That was a good idea. Let's wake up your Mom and get this day started."

"Don't bother, I'm already up," Sylvia said, walking into Josh's room. "In fact, I had a hard time sleeping. I was worried we might oversleep. How did you get dressed so quickly, Josh?"

"I slept in my clothes." Josh beamed, pulling on his shoes. "I don't want to miss a minute of this event."

"Yes, sir, captain, we'll soon be on our way," Aunt Louise mocked. "Hop to it, Sylvia."

"Will do. Be ready in a few minutes."

Josh put his binoculars in his backpack along with the sunscreen, umbrella, and camera. From the kitchen he added several packages of peanut butter crackers and a sausage biscuit. Aunt Louise joined him, wearing her wide-brimmed hat and walking boots. She made coffee for her thermos and put sandwiches and sodas into the cooler.

While Aunt Louise put the cooler in the car, Sylvia got the lawn chairs.

"Do we have everything?" Sylvia asked.

"Enough to camp out for a week," Aunt Louise answered.

Josh climbed into the back seat along with the cooler.

Mom sat up front with Aunt Louise. "Buckle up," she called to the back seat. "Three history seekers are off to the party."

Aunt Louise eased out the driveway. "Here we go."

The James Island Connector had more traffic than usual at such an early hour. Other history seekers were obviously headed to *the big show.*

The sun was just beginning to peep over the horizon as they crossed the Cooper River Bridge.

"Whoa, this is great. Just look at all those boats down there," Josh exclaimed. "I'll bet Scott is on one of them."

"Probably so," Mom replied. "They're expecting many private boats. The harbor is closed to commercial boats today."

Traffic became heavier as Aunt Louise drove onto Sullivan's Island. A long line of cars stretched toward the south end of the island. Following the crowd to Fort Moultrie, Aunt Louise took the last available parking space at the visitors center.

After crossing the street, they skirted the fort getting to the beach. Several hundred people were already there, but Aunt Louise and Mom managed to find a spot just big enough for the three of them.

Josh ate a sausage biscuit and drank orange juice. In their hurry, there had been no mention of breakfast. Josh had come prepared.

"Eating already?" asked Aunt Louise.

"Have some," he said.

"It does look like we're in for a wait. Might as well enjoy ourselves." Aunt Louise removed the lid from her thermos and joined Josh with her cup of coffee.

The air seemed electric with excitement. A group of women wore black Colonial-style dresses, portraying widows mourning the *Hunley* crew. Civil War re-enactors, dressed in Confederate uniforms, waved both the

American flag and the Confederate battle flag. In the sand, someone had written WELCOME HUNLEY!

While waiting, people watched portable televisions as the local stations gave play-by-play accounts of the raising.

Aunt Louise, Mom, and Josh watched the horizon through binoculars. The sun was now up and the air was growing warmer. Umbrellas went up for shade, and the viewing continued.

At 8:39 AM, the *H. L. Hunley* submarine broke the surface of the Atlantic Ocean, after 136 years. For a moment there was silence, and then a great outburst of shouts, whistles, and cheers. Hundreds saluted as the vessel was lifted fifteen feet into the air. Horns sounded from every direction. Back on the peninsula, a twenty-one-gun salute marked the event, and the sound of many ringing church bells traveled across the harbor.

Aunt Louise, Mom, and Josh stood at attention, waving their small flags. The three gave a salute in honor of this great day in history.

Josh was the first to speak. "I've got goose bumps."

"So have I," added Mom.

Aunt Louise wiped tears from her eyes. "The lost treasure has been found," she said.

Josh picked up his binoculars and took a closer look

at the *Hunley*. "It's smaller than I thought it would be."

"It does look small compared to the replicas," Aunt Louise said. "But the real irony is that something of such unique beauty could be a coffin!"

"I don't see how nine men could fit into that little thing," Josh said. "I hope they will soon get them out and bury them at Magnolia Cemetery."

"I'm sure the men will be given an honorable and proper military burial as quickly as possible," Mom responded. "At last, they will be united with the two other crews."

Aunt Louise, Mom, and Josh stood without talking, their eyes locked on the sub. Securely strapped in its lift truss, the *Hunley* was gently lowered onto the barge that would carry it safely to the Warren Lasch Conservation Center on the old navy base. To protect it from the atmosphere, the vessel was kept wet by a continuous spray of water from two ordinary garden sprinklers.

As they watched, the barge was tied to a tugboat, and the *Hunley* began the fifteen-mile ride to its new home. The procession was led by a Confederate color guard, carrying four flags: the American flag, the South Carolina flag, the Second National flag of the

Confederacy, and the Charleston Naval Squadron

flag. Police and more than 300 private boats followed
alongside and behind.

"What a breathtaking sight!" Aunt Louise exclaimed.

"It's magnificent," Mom whispered.

"It's awesome," Josh agreed.

Walking to the car, Josh said, "This has been a day to remember. I wish I could have seen the *Hunley* up closer. I really would like to touch it."

"You'll be able to see it later," responded Aunt Louise. "The Conservation Center is supposed to be opened to the public for limited observation of the *Hunley*. And we'll be first in line for tickets."

"Promise?"

"Scout's honor."

Getting into the car, Mom said, "Now it's time for the three history buffs to celebrate this memorable event with an all-American hotdog. I'm starving!"

"I'll have apple pie and ice cream for dessert," Aunt Louise said.

"I'll take peanuts and a box of Cracker Jacks," Josh added.

"What, no fireworks?" Aunt Louise joked.

With great emotion, Mom said, "We don't need fireworks for this celebration. We need only the true American spirit."

"And I have that," Josh said.

"And I have that," echoed Aunt Louise.

"Don't forget me. I have that, too!" Mom boasted.

Josh grinned. "And that makes three."

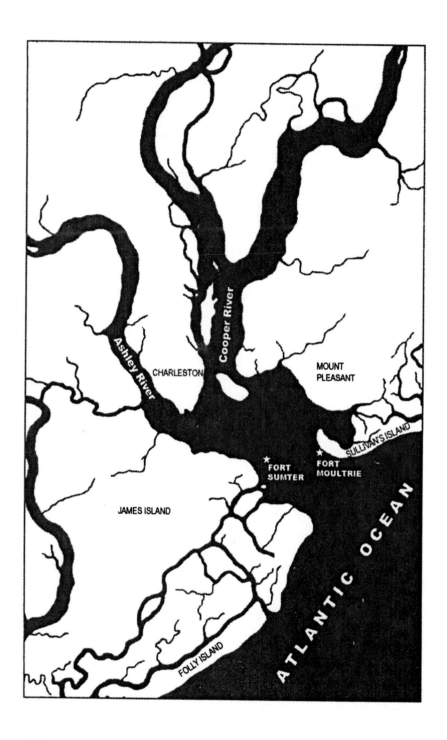

Timeline

Spring 1863
The *Hunley* was built in Mobile, Alabama, by James McClintock, Baxter Watson, and Horace Hunley.

August 1863
The *Hunley* submarine was transported to Charleston.

August 29, 1863
Five crew members drowned in the first recorded training mission of the CSS *H. L. Hunley*. Their names were Frank Doyle, John Kelly, Michael Cane, Nicholas Davis, and Absolum Williams. They were buried in a marina's cemetery on the outskirts of Charleston.

October 15, 1863
The Hunley and Park crew died in a test run. Crew members included Robert Brockbank, Joseph Patterson, Henry Beard, Charles L. Sprague, Charles McHugh, John Marshall, Thomas Park, and Captain Horace L. Hunley. They were buried in Magnolia Cemetery in Charleston.

February 17, 1864
The third crew of the *Hunley*, known as the Dixon Crew, set sail. Crew members included Lt. George E. Dixon (who served as captain), Arnold Becker, F. Collins, a Mr. Miller, Capt. Joseph Ridgway, C. Simkins, C. F. Carlson, James A. Wicks, and a ninth man believed to be a Mr. White. That same evening, the *Hunley*'s torpedo sank the Union ship *Housatonic*. The submarine seemed to have disappeared in the explosion and crew members went down with the vessel.

The *Hunley* was the first submarine to sink a ship in wartime. This feat was not achieved again until 1917, during World War I.

1889

United Daughters of the Confederacy erected a memorial at White Point Gardens honoring *Hunley* crew members.

1947

Bodies of the Hunley's first crew were discovered, buried in an old cemetery for Confederate sailors, during excavation on the Citadel campus while building the Johnson Hagood Stadium.

1967

The *Hunley* Museum opened on Broad Street in Charleston.

1969

The *Hunley* Museum closed. Artifacts were relocated to the Charleston Museum, at the corner of Rutledge Avenue and Calhoun Street.

May 1995

The *Hunley* submarine was discovered during a diving expedition led by Clive Cussler. The vessel was nestled in sand in twenty-seven feet of water approximately four miles off the coast of Sullivan's Island, just outside Charleston Harbor.

1999

Turner Network Television broadcast *The Hunley*, a full-length, made-for-television movie depicting the last voyage of the fated submarine. The movie was filmed in Charleston.

March 25, 2000

Bodies of the crew from the first training mission were reinterred in Magnolia Cemetery in Charleston. An elaborate procession, with reenactors dressed in Colonial garb, bore the bodies by horse-drawn carriage through downtown. The men were given a formal burial with full military honors.

May 2000
The diving crew began the task of bringing the *Hunley* to the surface.

May 12, 2000
Charleston Post & Courier reported that the site excavation was beginning. "Divers will vacuum sand . . . and begin dredging a trough around the *Hunley*."

May 17, 2000
The top of the submarine was exposed.

August 8, 2000
The diving crew lifted the *Hunley* from the water. It was placed on a barge and taken to a conservation center at the old Charleston navy base for further study and preservation. It could take five to seven years before it is ready to be placed in the Charleston Museum.

September 2000
The Warren Lasch Conservation Center, the *Hunley's* temporary home, was opened for public viewing, by appointment, of the submarine.

At a future time
Plans are being made for construction of a new building at the Charleston Museum to permanently house the *H. L. Hunley* and relics now in storage at the Museum.

Select Bibliography

Burton, E. Milby. *Siege of Charleston, 1861-1865*. Columbia: University of South Carolina Press, 1970.

Campbell, R. Thomas. *The CSS H. L. Hunley, Confederate Submarine*. Shippensburg, PA: Burd Street Press, 2000.

———. *Gray Thunder*. Shippensburg, PA: Mane Publishing Company, Inc., 1996.

Coker, PC III. *Charleston's Maritime Heritage, 1865*. Charleston, SC: CokerCraft Press, 1987.

Cussler, Clive. *The Sea Hunters*. New York: Pocket Star Books, 1996.

Davis, B. *The Civil War: Strange & Fascinating Facts*. New York: Fairfax Press, 1983.

Jones, Virgil C. *The Civil War at Sea*, Volumes I, II, III. New York: Holt Rinehart & Winston, 1960-62.

Kloeppel, James E. *Danger Beneath the Waves: A History of the Confederate Submarine, The H. L. Hunley*. Orangeburg, SC: Sandlapper Publishing, Inc., 1987.

Ragan, Mark K. *The Hunley: Submarines, Sacrifice, & Success in the Civil War*. Charleston, SC: Narwhal Press, Inc., 1995, 2000.

———. *Union and Confederate Submarine Warfare in the Civil War*. Mason City, IA: Savas Publishing, 1999.

Spencer, E. Lee. *Treasures of the Confederate Coast: The Real*

Rhett Butler & Other Revelations. Charleston, SC: Narwhal Press, 1995.

Teaster, Gerald F. *The Confederate Submarine, H. L. Hunley.* Summerville, SC: Junior History Press, 1980.

Wilcox, Arthur M. *The Civil War at Charleston.* Charleston, SC: *Post & Courier,* 1966.

Museum Video: *Rebel Beneath the Waves.* Stuart Television Productions, Concord, MA.

Movie: *The Hunley,* Turner Network Television, 1999.

Leon B. (Buddy) Ward III, tugboat captain/writer, Charleston, SC. Interview by the author.

Dawn Hammer Davis, Lead Park Ranger, National Park Service, Fort Sumter National Monument, Charleston, SC. Interview by the author.

"Nautilus Gets Papers on Confederate *Hunley,*" *Charleston News & Courier,* January 25, 1958.

"Salvage of Submarine Hunley Has Chance for Success," *Charleston News & Courier,* June 18, 1957.

"The *Hunley* Project," *Charleston Post & Courier,* May–August 2000.

"The *Hunley,*" supplement to the *Charleston Post & Courier,* February 21, 1999.

Web Site: www.hunley.org — Friends of the Hunley

Author MARGIE WILLIS CLARY is a teacher and professional storyteller. She holds a masters degree in education and taught elementary school for thirty years. Her first book of fiction, *A Sweet, Sweet Basket*, was listed among *Smithsonian* Magazine's "Notable Books for Children, 1995." She published her second children's storybook, *Searching the Lights*, in 1998. At that time, she also released a small color guidebook to the lighthouses in South Carolina called *Carolina Lights*. *Make It Three: The Story of the CSS H. L. Hunley, Civil War Submarine* is her first chapter book.

Ms. Clary lives in Charleston, South Carolina. She and her husband, Ralph, have two children and three grandchildren.

Ms. Clary is a member of the National Association of Storytellers and the Society of Children's Book Writers and Illustrators. She is on the approved artist roster of the South Carolina Arts Commission.

Illustrator BECKY HYATT RICKENBAKER is a graduate of the Art Institute of Atlanta and has worked as an illustrator and graphic designer for twenty years. In that time she has created artwork for magazines, newspapers and a variety of clients. Her painting of a peregrine falcon was selected as the South Carolina Wildlife Federation's print of the year in 1992. She lives with her family in Lexington, South Carolina.

Printed in the United States
97330LV00001B/259-405/A

9 780878 441587